LOOK AND FIND®

THOMAS & FRIENDS™

Illustrated by S.I. International

Thomas the Tank Engine & Friends™

A BRITT ALLCROFT PRODUCTION

Based on The Railway Series by The Reverend W Awdry. © 2007 Gullane (Thomas) LLC
Thomas the Tank Engine & Friends and Thomas & Friends are trademarks of Gullane (Thomas) Limited.
Thomas the Tank Engine and Friends and Design is Reg. U.S. Pat. & Tm. Off.
A HIT Entertainment Company.

Published by Louis Weber, C.E.O., Publications International, Ltd.
7373 North Cicero Avenue, Lincolnwood, Illinois 60712
Ground Floor, 59 Gloucester Place, London W1U 8JJ

Customer Service: 1-800-595-8484 or customer_service@pilbooks.com

www.pilbooks.com

publications international, ltd.

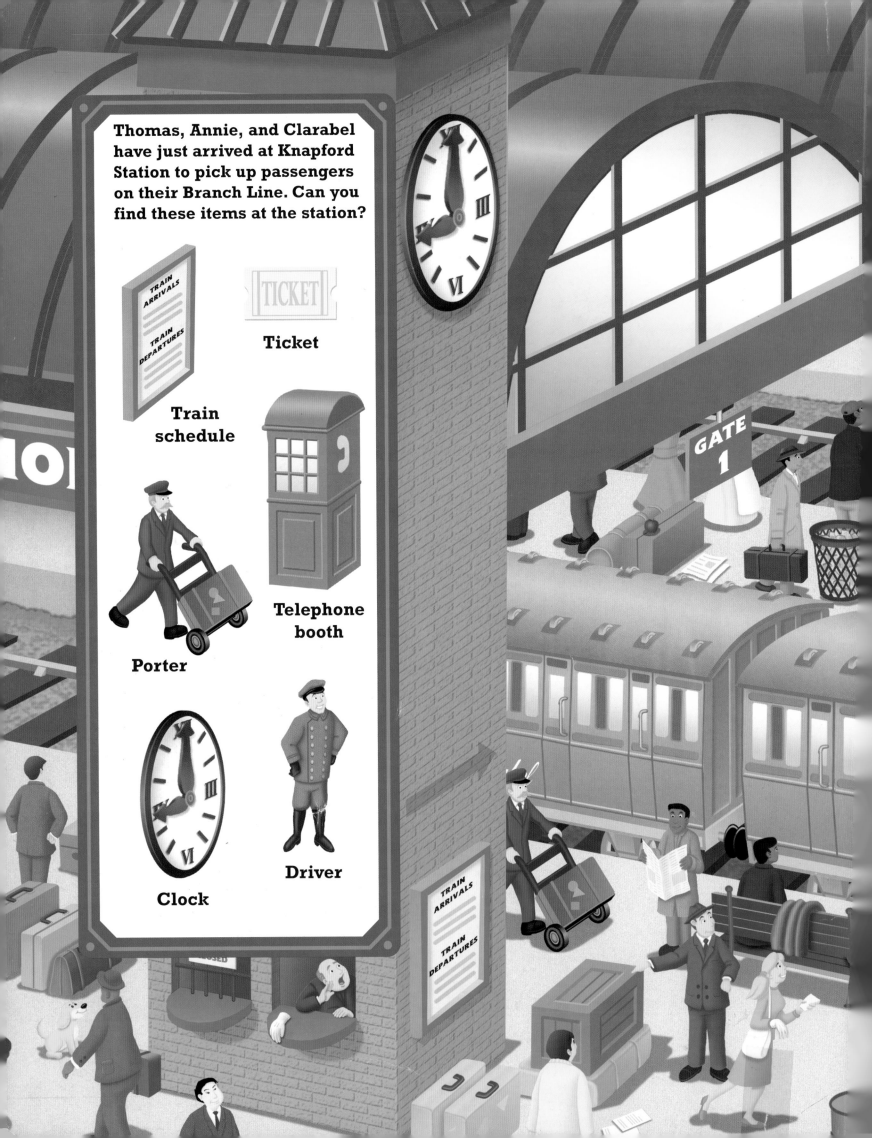

Thomas, Annie, and Clarabel have just arrived at Knapford Station to pick up passengers on their Branch Line. Can you find these items at the station?

Train schedule

Ticket

Porter

Telephone booth

Clock

Driver

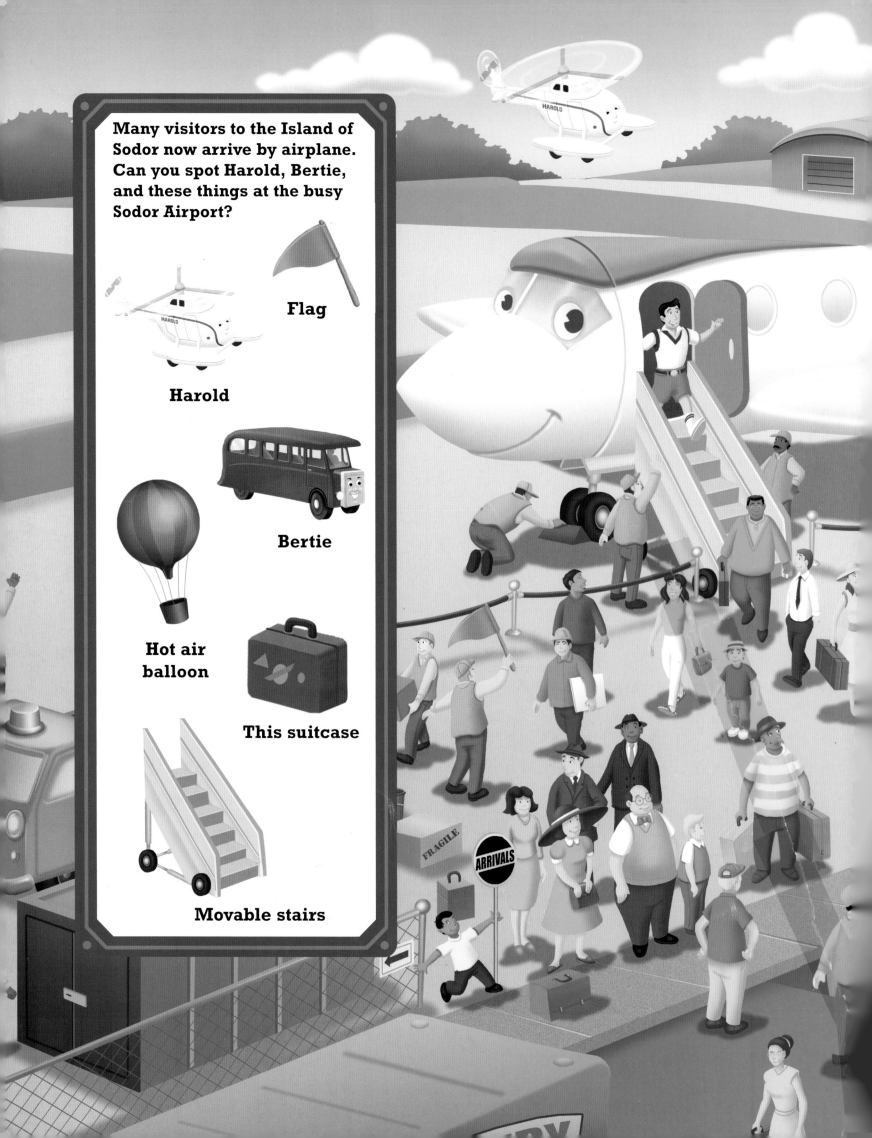

Many visitors to the Island of Sodor now arrive by airplane. Can you spot Harold, Bertie, and these things at the busy Sodor Airport?

Flag

Harold

Bertie

Hot air balloon

This suitcase

Movable stairs

Thomas is collecting fresh milk at Farmer McColl's farm. Can you spot these things on the farm?

Ear of corn

Rooster

Cow

Shovel

Scarecrow

Terence

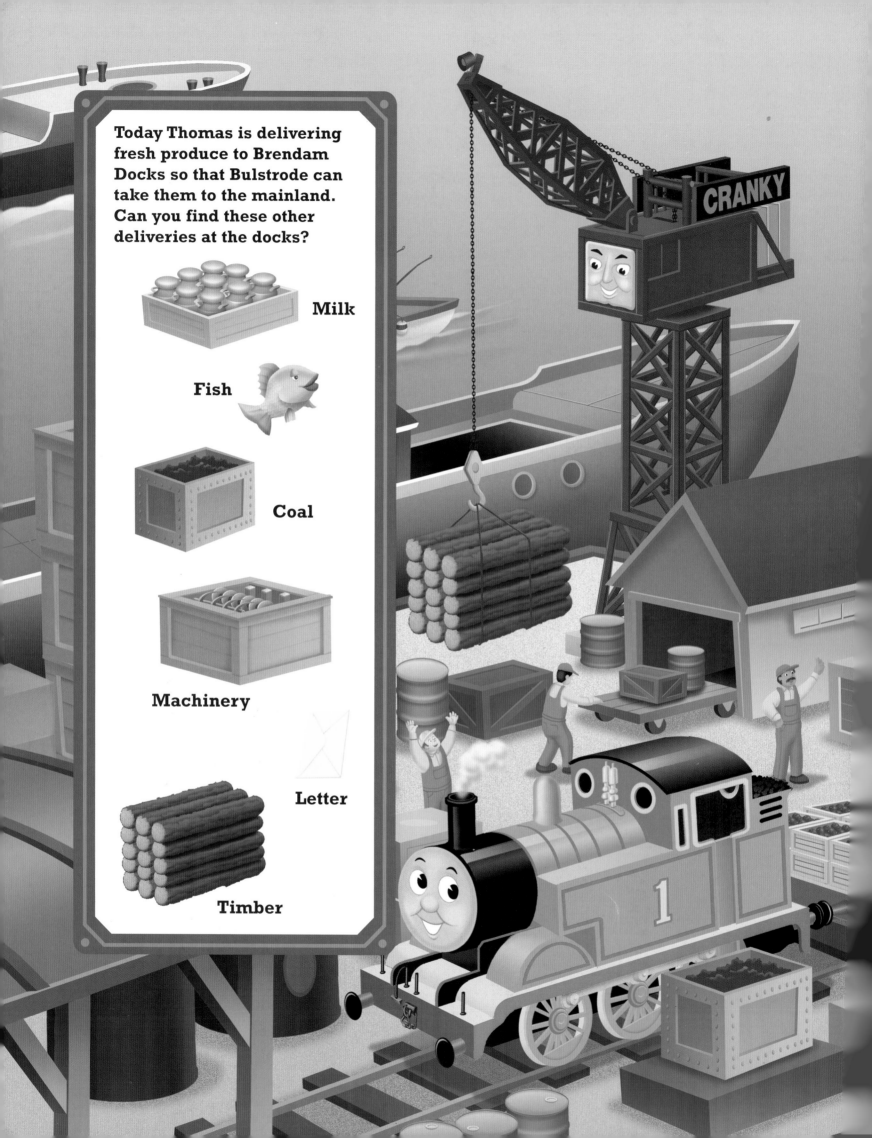

Today Thomas is delivering fresh produce to Brendam Docks so that Bulstrode can take them to the mainland. Can you find these other deliveries at the docks?

Milk

Fish

Coal

Machinery

Letter

Timber

CRANKY

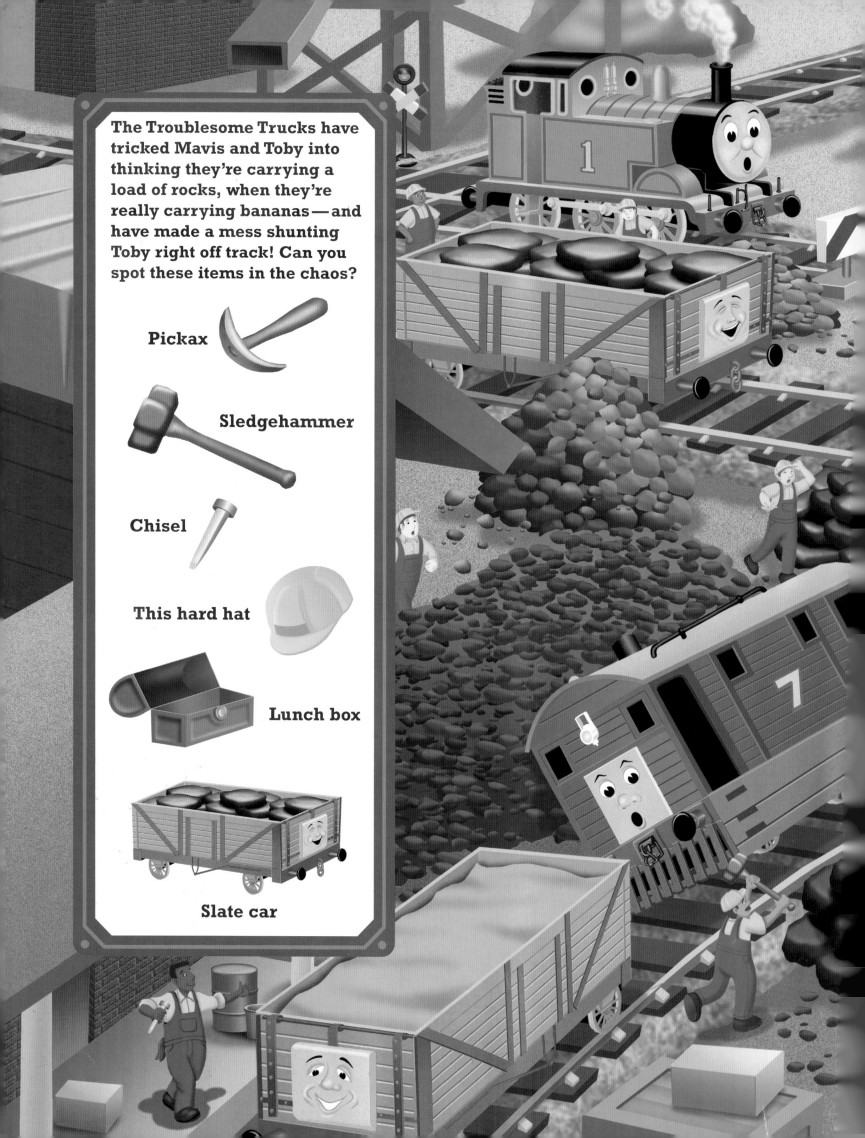

The Troublesome Trucks have tricked Mavis and Toby into thinking they're carrying a load of rocks, when they're really carrying bananas — and have made a mess shunting Toby right off track! Can you spot these items in the chaos?

Pickax

Sledgehammer

Chisel

This hard hat

Lunch box

Slate car

The circus has come to Sodor! Thomas is helping carry supplies to the Fairgrounds. Can you find these parts of the circus celebration?

Show dogs

This performer

Barker

Peanuts

Trapeze artist

Barbells

Thomas is at the train yard waiting for Sir Topham Hatt to finish his lunch and give him instructions on his next job. Take a peek in Sir Topham Hatt's office and see if you can find these items:

Telephone

Lady Hatt

Pocket watch

Top hat

Handkerchief

Map of the railway

It's a great day for the seaside. Thomas gets to carry his favorite passengers — the children of Sodor! Can you find these items?

This blanket

Ball

Kite

Ice cream cone

Balloon

Sandcastle

Knapford Station is buzzing with people bustling about. Can you find these items that passengers have left behind?

- ☐ Glove
- ☐ Eyeglasses
- ☐ Apple
- ☐ Flowers
- ☐ Red coat
- ☐ Umbrella

People are coming from far and wide to the Island of Sodor, and the airport has never been busier! Can you spot these visiting vacationers?

- ☐ A woman wearing a yellow sun hat
- ☐ A man wearing a white vest
- ☐ A boy on a bicycle
- ☐ A woman carrying a picnic basket
- ☐ A girl with a tennis racket
- ☐ A man eating an ice-cream cone

Farmer McColl grows a rainbow of fruits and vegetables. Go back to the farm and find these other colorful things.

- ☐ Red wheelbarrow
- ☐ Orange peppers
- ☐ Farmer McColl's yellow hat
- ☐ Green rake
- ☐ Purple eggplants
- ☐ Gray horse

There is always plenty to do at Brendam Docks. Can you lend a hand and find these useful vehicles?

- ☐ A barge (Bulstrode)
- ☐ A diesel train engine (Salty)
- ☐ A crane (Cranky)
- ☐ A cart
- ☐ A fishing boat
- ☐ A bus (Bertie)

The Troublesome Trucks are driving everyone at the quarry bananas! Without slipping, can you count twenty-five of the yellow fruits?

25

Before the Big Tent action begins, head back to the Fairground and search for these circus animals:

❑ Elephant

❑ Monkey

❑ Lion

❑ Tiger

❑ Bear

❑ Horse

Everyone counts on Sir Topham Hatt. Help him keep things on track by finding these numbers in his office:

❑ 1 ❑ 2

❑ 3 ❑ 4

❑ 5 ❑ 6

Dive back into the seaside scene to find these animals and insects. But don't forget your sunscreen!

❑ Dog

❑ Starfish

❑ Cow

❑ Butterfly

❑ Dragon

❑ Bumblebee

Can you find this puppy in every scene?